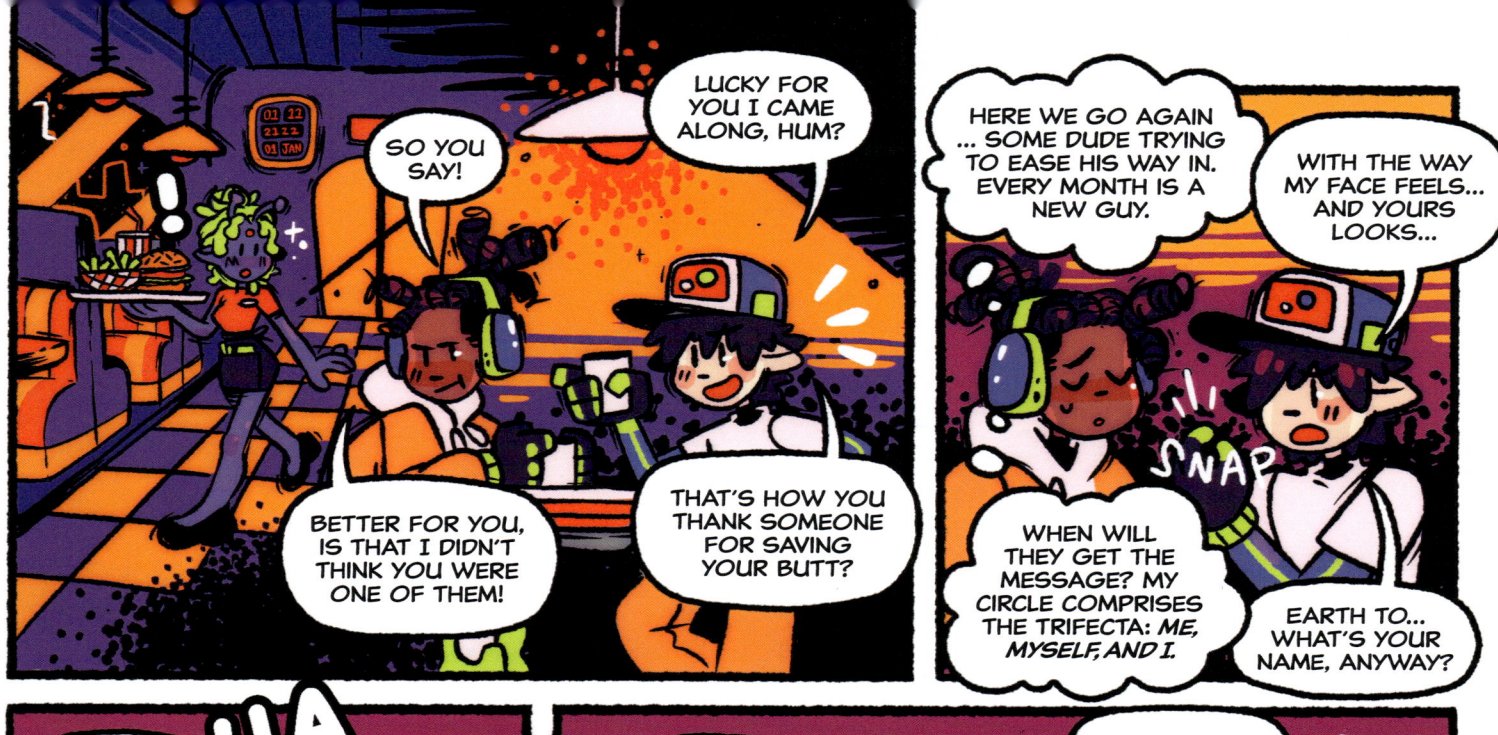

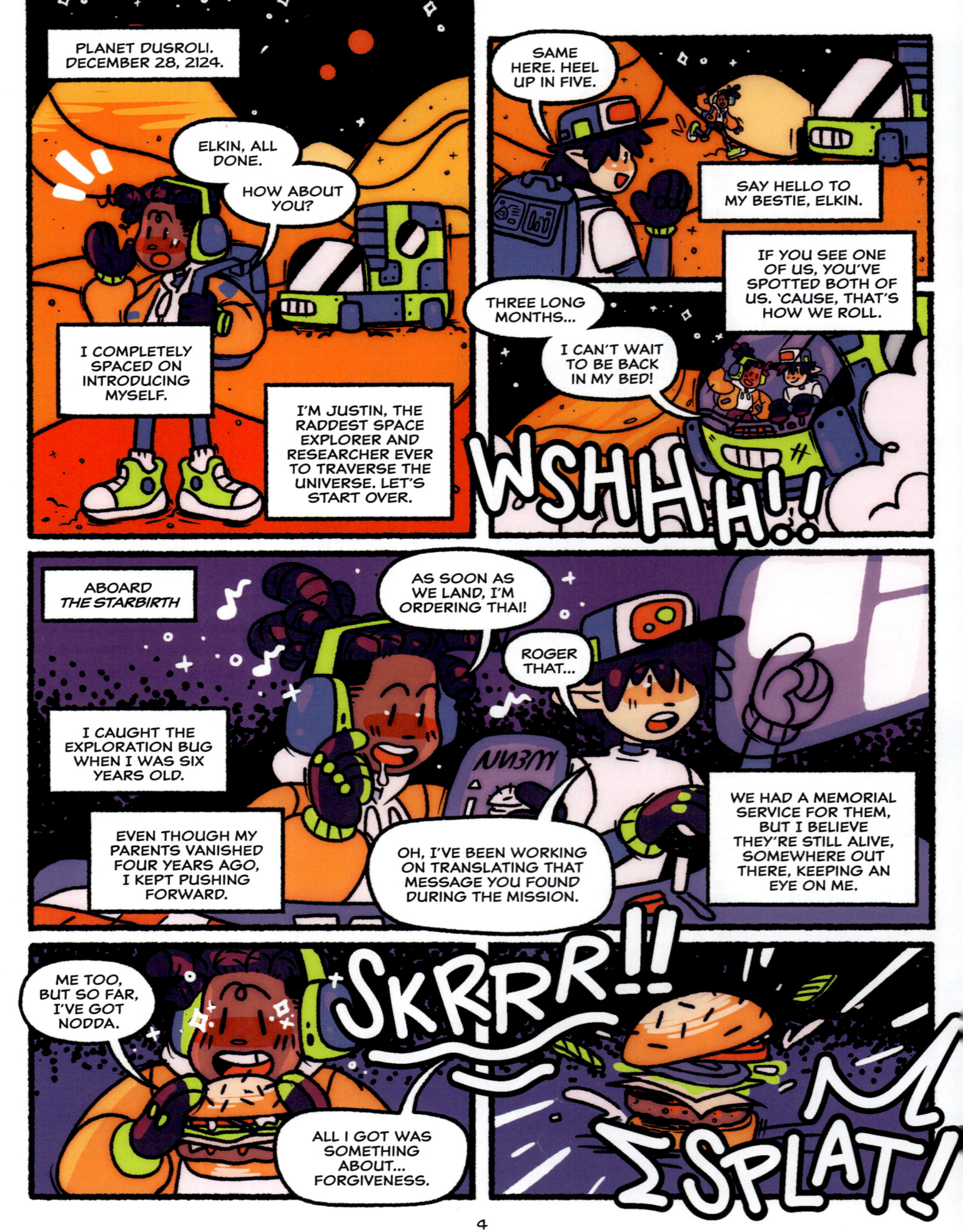

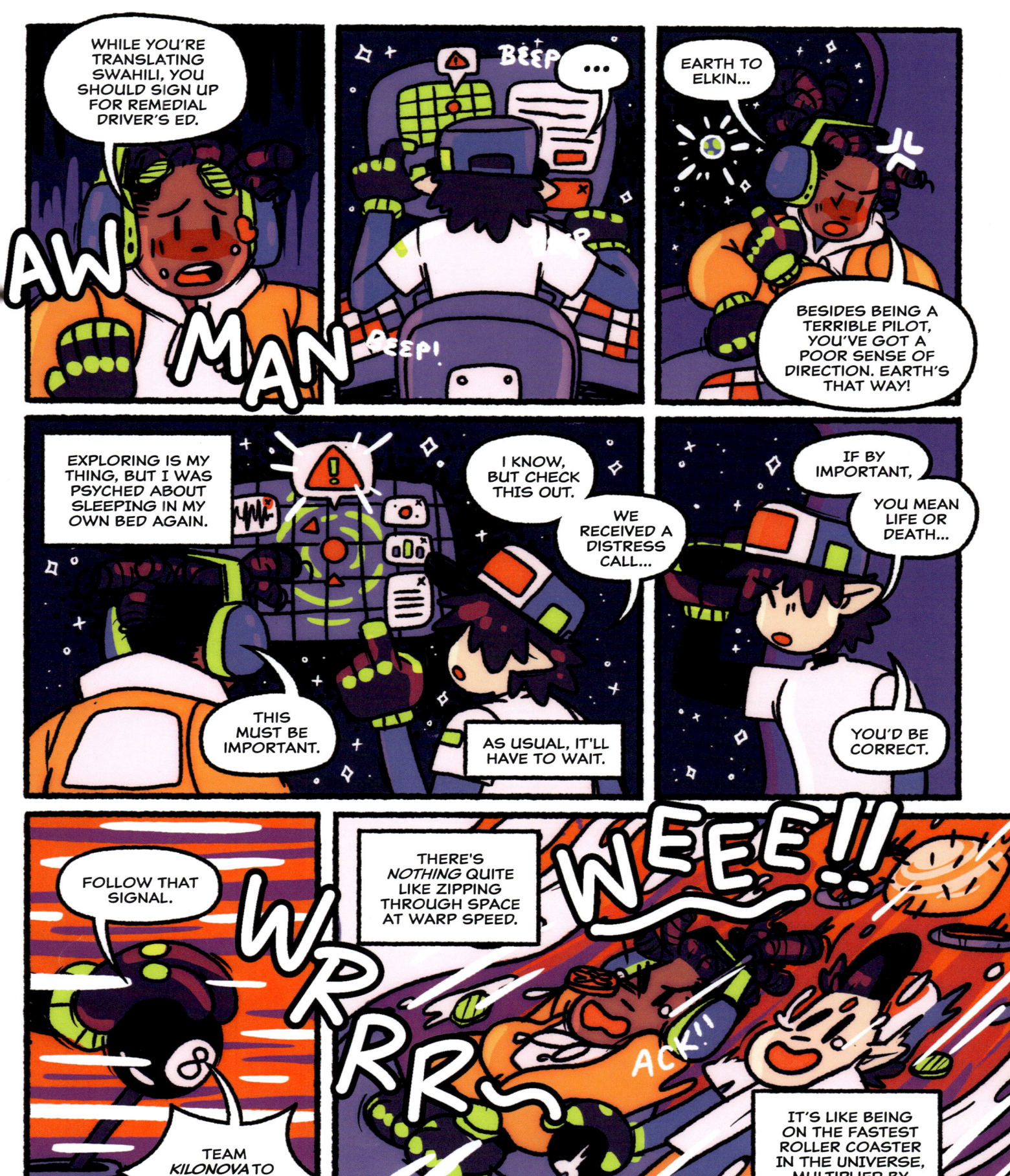

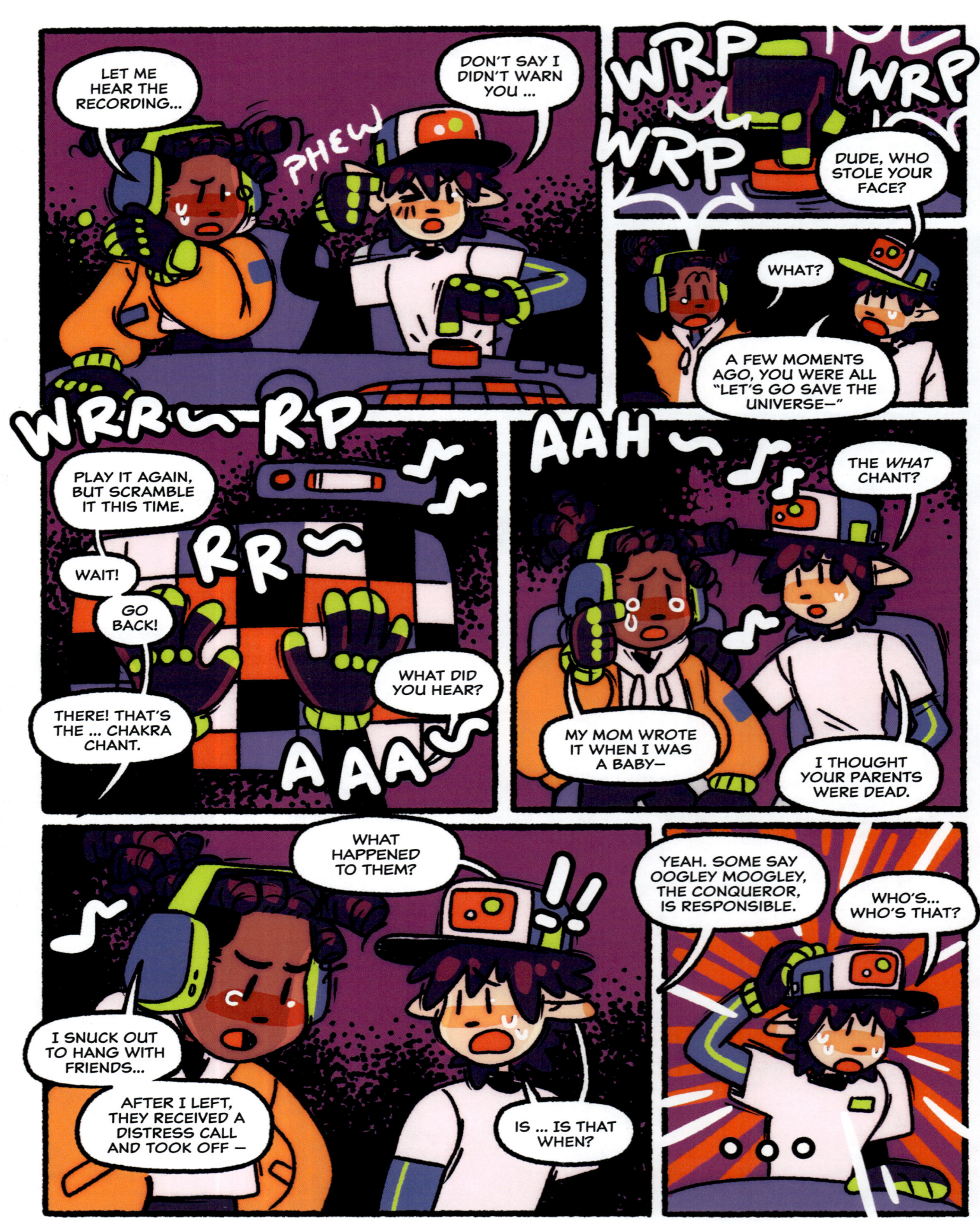

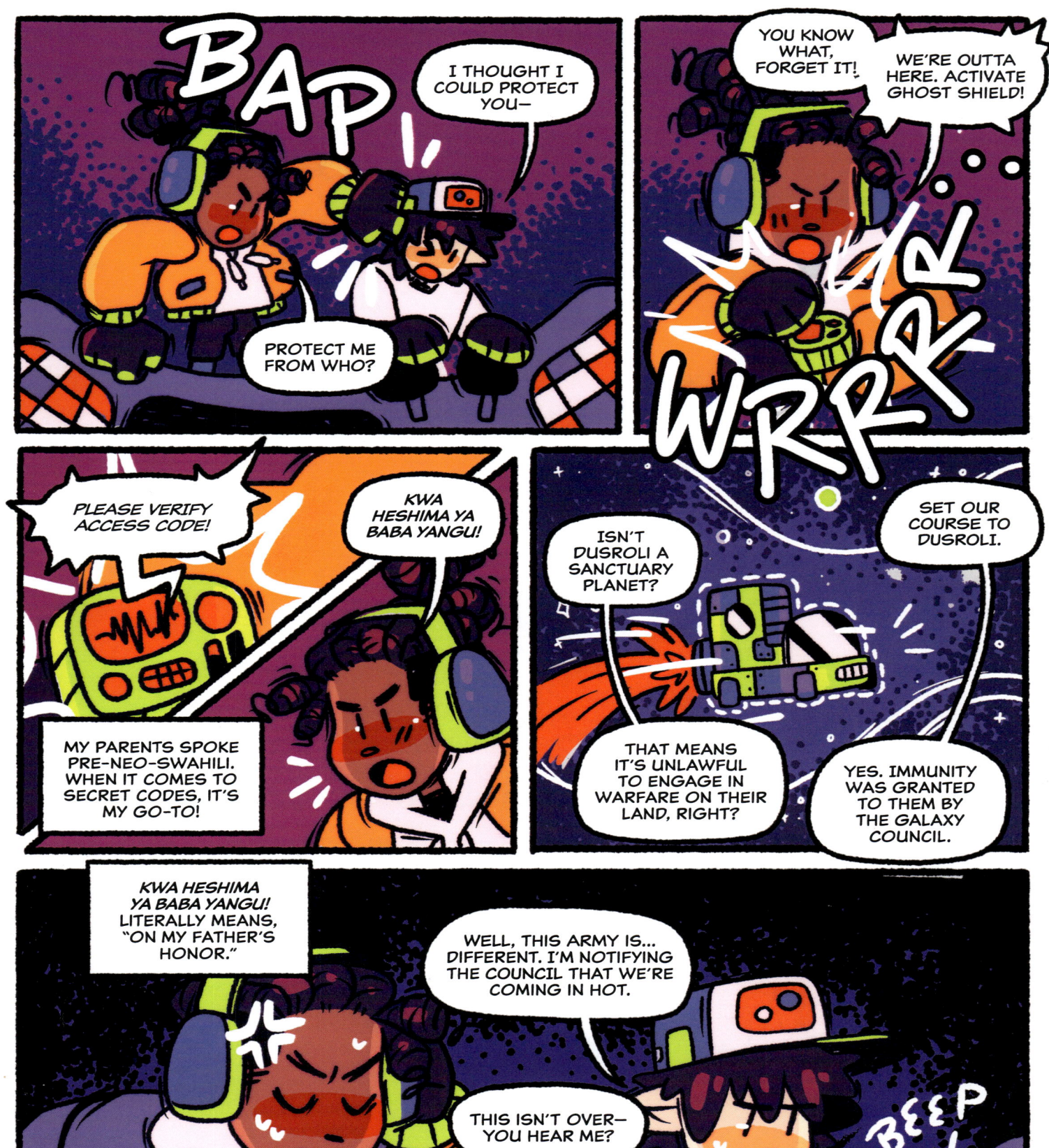

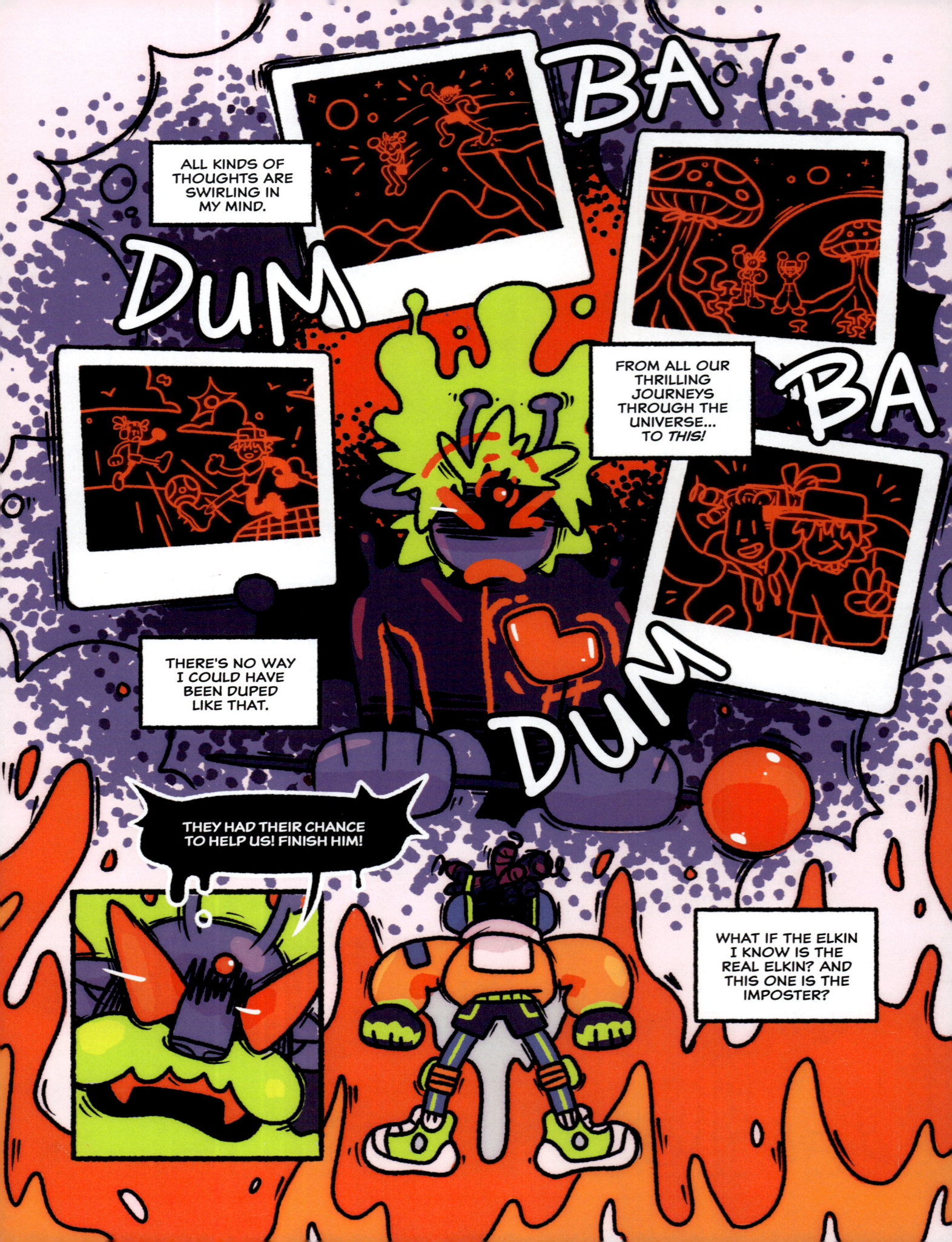

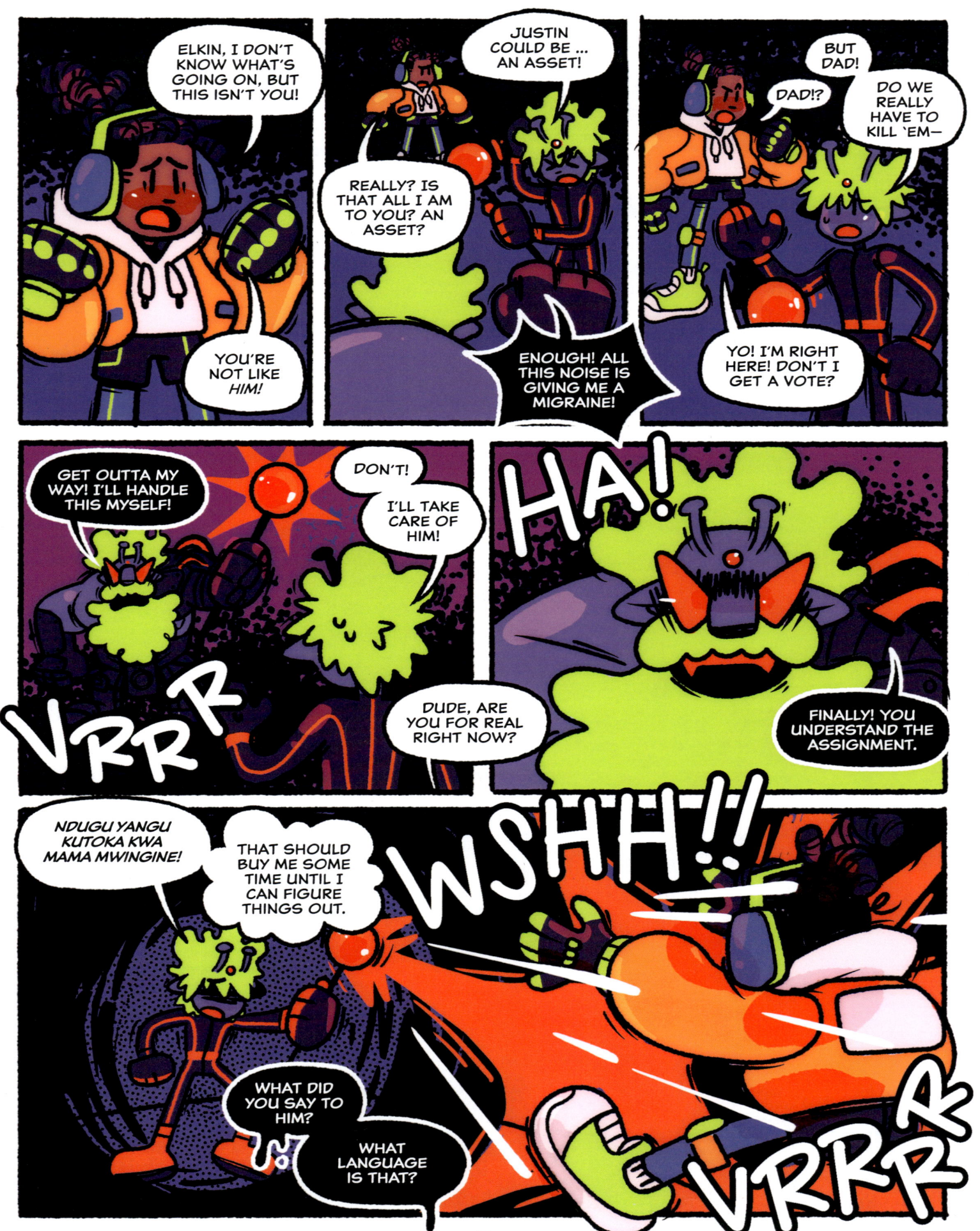

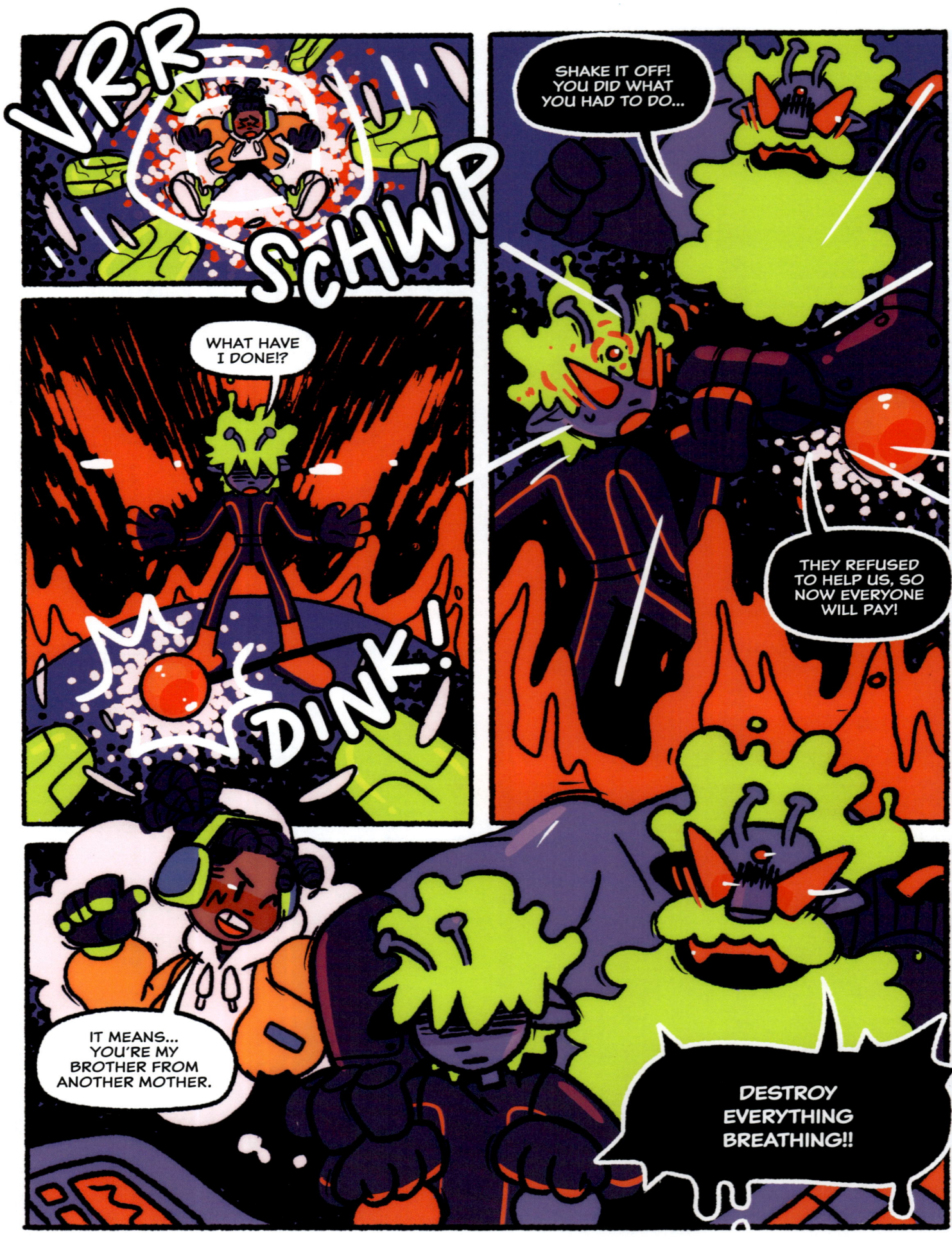

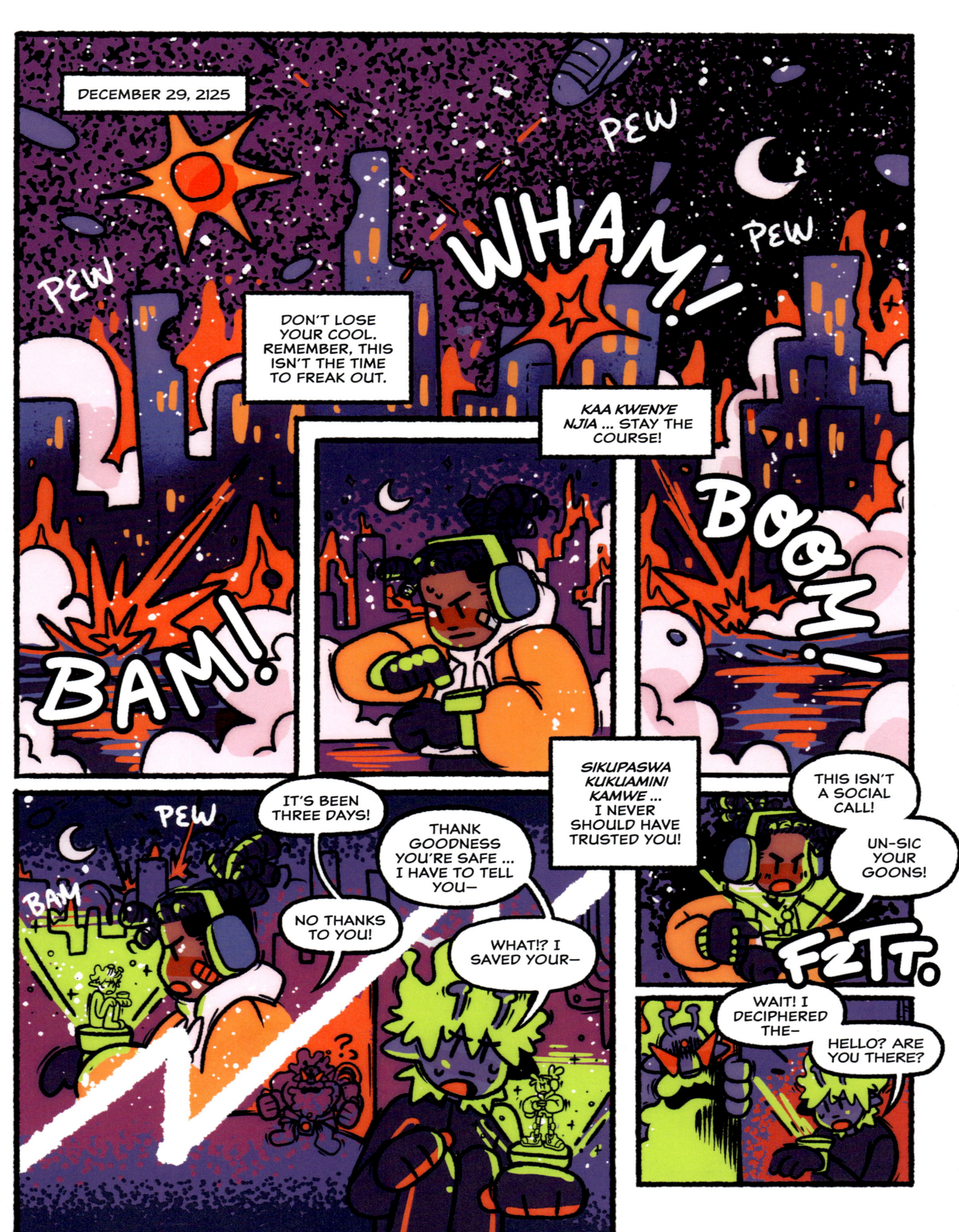

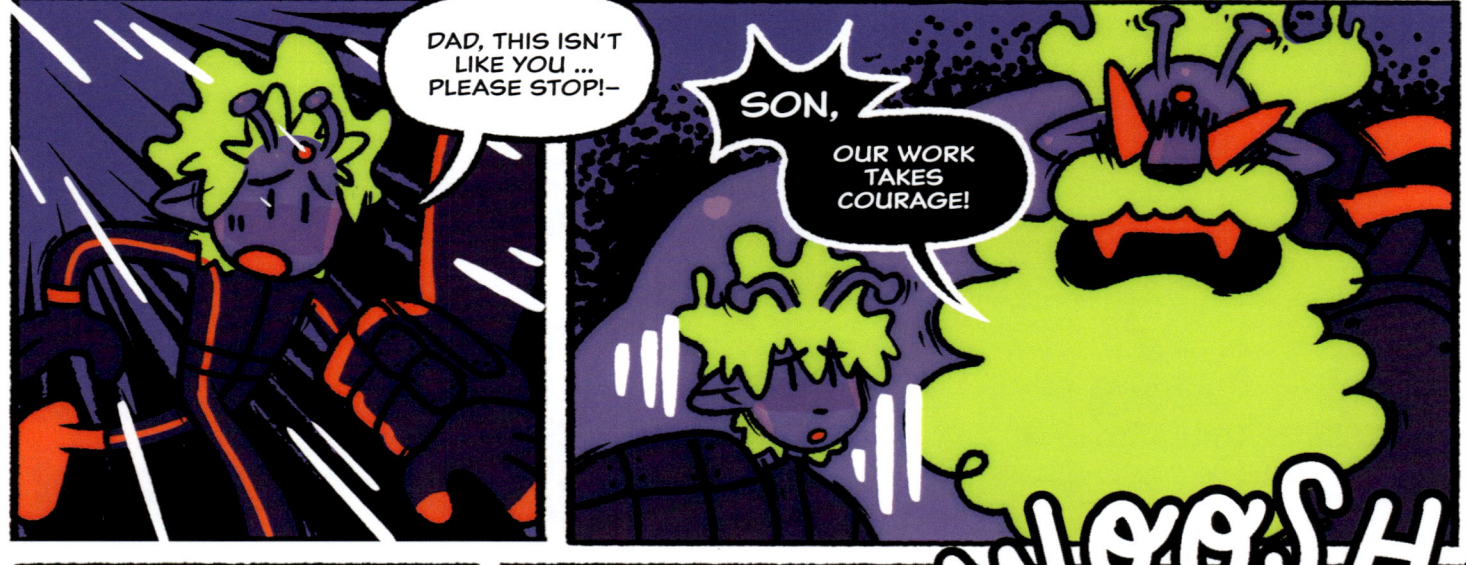

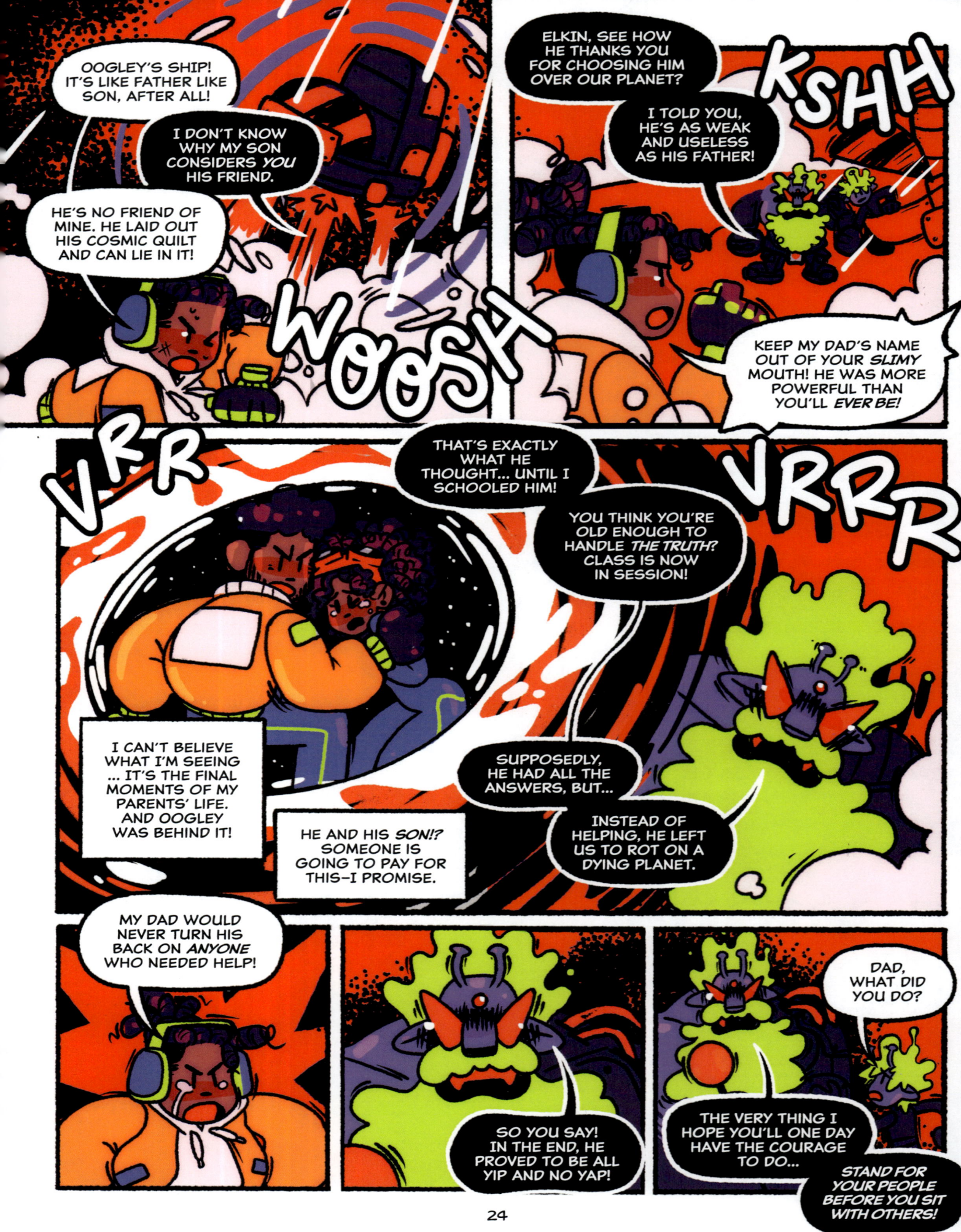

HA! HA! HA!! HA!! HA!! HA!

TO THINK I ACTUALLY ONCE FEARED YOU—OR YOUR FATHER!!

EL... DID YOU KNOW ABOUT THIS?

DUDE, NO WAY!

OOGLEY MOOGLEY, YOU WILL PAY FOR WHAT YOU'VE DONE!

HA HA HA HA

HE'S... HE'S...

...RIGHT!

HEADS UP, MY MAN!

HOW IS THIS EVEN REAL? I'M GROWING STRONGER, TALLER, MORE POWERFUL! MAYBE I CAN DEFEAT THAT SLIMESTER AFTER ALL...

WHOA! WHAT'S HAPPENING!?

HUH?

KSHHHH

WHAT HAVE YOU DONE?!

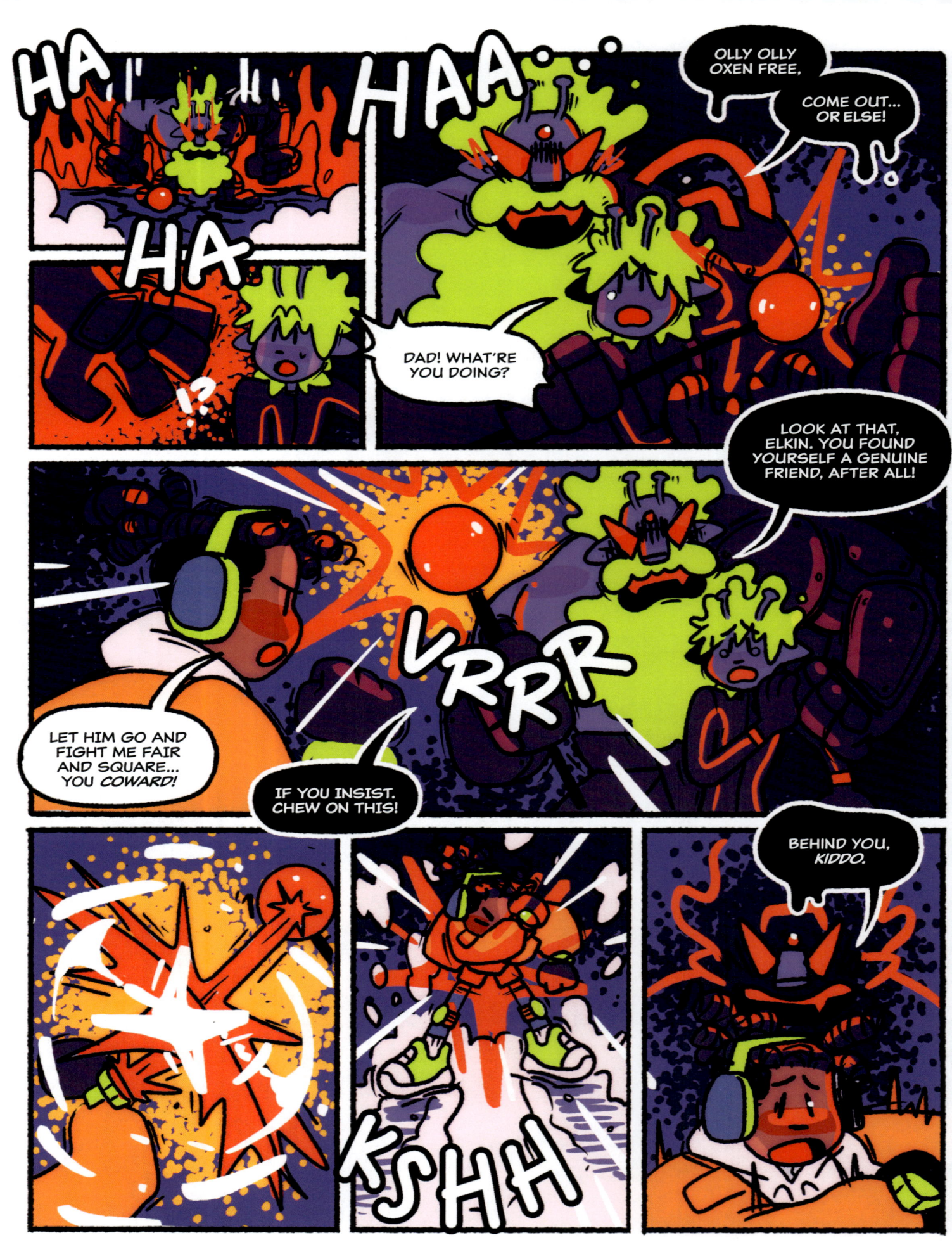

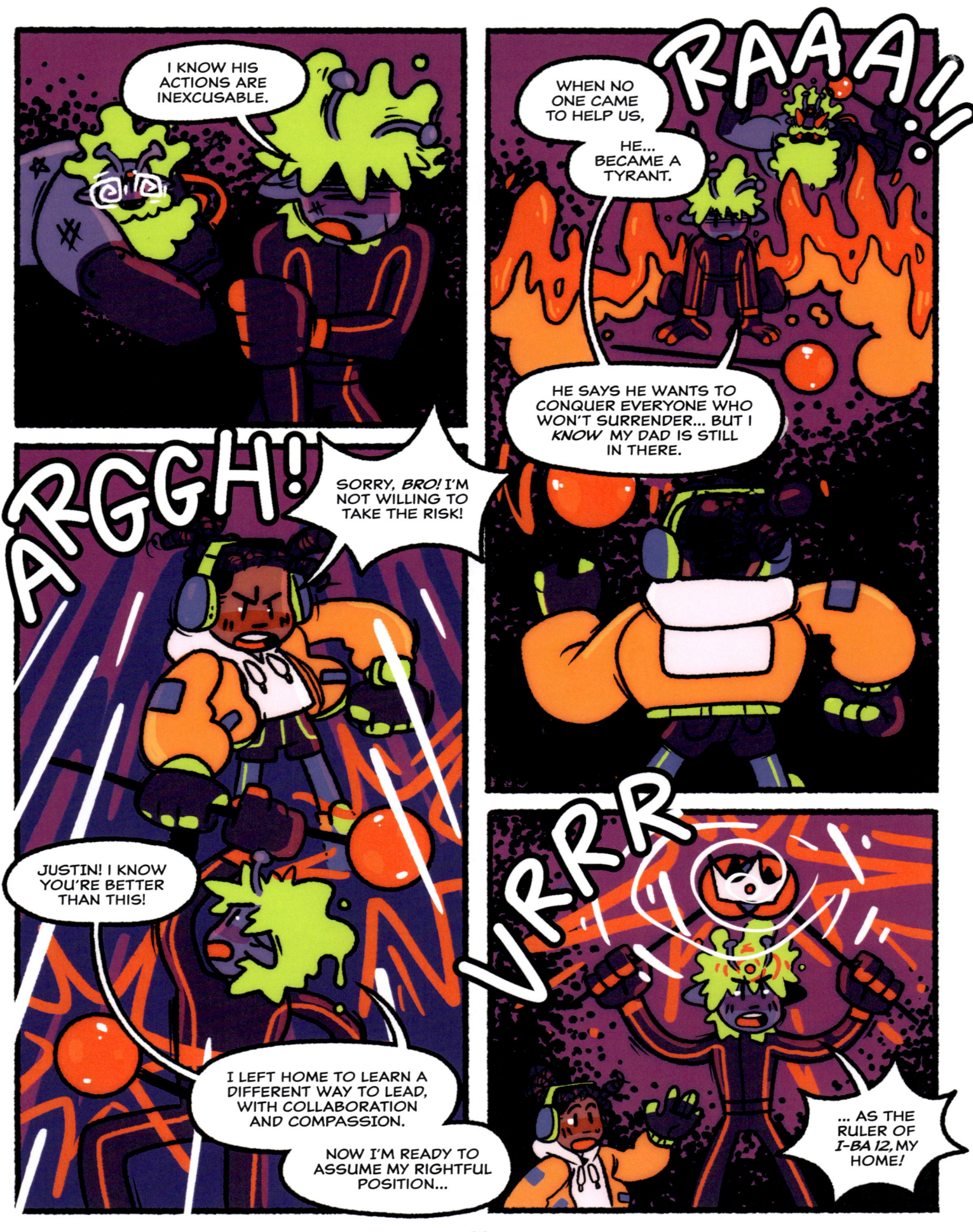

THIS IS A WORK OF FICTION. NAMES, CHARACTERS, PLACES, AND INCIDENTS EITHER ARE THE PRODUCT OF THE AUTHOR'S IMAGINATION OR ARE USED FICTITIOUSLY.

ANY RESEMBLANCE TO ACTUAL PERSONS, LIVING OR DEAD, EVENTS, OR LOCALES IS ENTIRELY COINCIDENTAL.

TEXT COPYRIGHT © 2024 FLORENZA LEE
ILLUSTRATION COPYRIGHT © 2024 ABIGAIL WATSON
SPECIAL THANKS TO BIXIE MATHIEU

JUSTIN SAVES THE UNIVERSE
PUBLISHED BY JESSE BYRD CREATIVE INC.
ALL RIGHTS RESERVED

NO PART OF THIS BOOK MAY BE REPRODUCED OR TRANSMITTED IN ANY FORM OR BY ANY MEANS WITHOUT WRITTEN PERMISSION FROM JESSE BYRD CREATIVE INC.

ISBN: 979-8-9895736-2-2